Party of the Butterflies

Natalie Frazier

Artist–A.H. Long

ISBN 978-1-63844-974-4 (paperback)
ISBN 978-1-63844-975-1 (digital)

Christian Faith Publishing, Inc.
832 Park Avenue
Meadville, PA 16335
www.christianfaithpublishing.com

Printed in the United States of America

To my imaginative and creative children, nephews and nieces. Bella, Jack, Lincoln, Andy, Aaron, Olivia, Jayden, Ellee and Rhett—you are all fearfully and wonderfully made by the creator of the heavens and the earth (Psalms 139).

On a bright sunny day with big fluffy clouds in the sky, grass on the ground, and a stream nearby, flowers are blooming, getting ready for the bees to gather their pollen to make honey with ease.

2

The butterflies slowly come out of their cocoons and flutter toward a beautiful garden on a hill for a party happening soon.

4

This garden was full of all kinds of flowers, vegetables, and fruits and a tall honeysuckle tower.

The most beautiful garden the butterflies had ever seen, it was the best place to have a party, a butterfly party indeed!

8

The butterflies hopped and fluttered from flower to flower and enjoyed the nectar from the tall honeysuckle tower.

10

Ladybugs, inchworms, crickets, and snails all came to watch the butterfly party in the most beautiful garden up on the hill.

12

As the bright sunlight was fading from up in the sky, the butterflies began their whispering goodbyes.

14

They hopped and fluttered from flower to flower, getting one last taste of that tall honeysuckle tower.

Their tummies were full as they whispered their goodbyes, and some were so full they couldn't even fly.

It was the most beautiful garden the butterflies had ever seen, and it was the perfect place for their butterfly party—and a party it was indeed!

The End

21

About the Author

Natalie Frazier is a Texas loving wife and mother to three beautiful young children. She is a retired hairstylist and an avid baker. Looking at her children's art on the refrigerator one evening, she felt the Lord calling her to write a children's book that allowed for the child to become the illustrator of the story. This is Natalie's first book, but she hopes to go on to write many more Imagine and Draw books in the future.